[美] 玛丽·波·奥斯本

01

DINOSAURS BEFORE DARK

恐龙谷历险记

主译：蓝葆春　蓝纯

湖北长江出版集团

湖北少年儿童出版社

★ 名人推荐 ★

陈乃芳：美国麻省大学高级访问学者，曾任驻比利时使馆兼驻欧盟使团教育处参赞，北京外国语大学校长；第九、十届全国政协委员，政协外事委员会委员，中国高等教育学会高教管理研究会副理事长，中国教育国际交流协会常务理事，《国际论坛》杂志主编；由泰国王储授予名誉教育学博士、由英国兰卡斯特大学校长亚历山大公主授予名誉法学博士，并有多部论著。

亲爱的少年读者们：

你们好！最近我有机会阅读了一套英汉双语版的系列丛书，名字叫做《神奇树屋》(Magic Tree House)，作者是当今美国最著名的少儿读物作家之一——玛丽·波·奥斯本。几乎全美国的少年儿童都喜欢读她写的《神奇树屋》，把她当作自己的好朋友。我虽早已年过六旬，但是我和美国的小朋友们一样，一拿到这套书就爱不释手，不到两天就全部读完了。

你们也许要问：您为什么这么喜欢这套书呢？

我的回答是：首先，作者的创作思路紧紧扣住了小读者渴求知识、喜欢冒险、充满好奇和富于幻想的心理特点，成功地打造了神奇树屋这个平台。神奇树屋挂在森林里最高的一棵橡树的顶上，里面堆满了图书。它的神奇之处在于小读者翻开其中的任何一本书，指着书中的一幅插图许愿说"我希望到那里去"，梦想就能即刻实现。其次，作者充分发挥"魔法"的作用，轻松自如地引领读者穿越时空，周游世界。从见识白垩纪恐龙时的翼龙和冰河时代最凶猛的野兽剑齿虎，到体察今日的澳洲袋鼠；从了解美国早期荒凉西部的牛仔生活，到欣赏古代中国牛郎织女的传奇故事；从游览古埃及的金字塔到身陷2000多年前中国的秦始皇陵；从遭遇加勒比海的海盗到幸会东方的日本忍者；从历险维苏威火山的爆发到探秘亚马孙河的热带雨林……真是随心所欲，神游八方。再者，作者成功地塑造了杰克和安妮这一对小兄妹，通过他俩的所见、所闻、所思、所想和亲身历险，把历史故事、神话传说、科普知识、人文传统等栩栩如生地展现在读者面前，让你如同身临其境。最后，这套书不仅内容丰富有趣，而且文字浅显易懂，让人捧读之下，不忍释手。

为了把这套优秀的少儿读物介绍给全中国的中小学生，湖北少儿出版社特别邀请了我的老同学、老同事、老朋友蓝葆春爷爷和他的女儿——北京外国语大学的蓝纯教授负责全套丛书的汉语翻译。他们的译文既忠实于原文，又琅琅上口。所以我建议小读者们在阅读过程中先读译文，再读原文，这样一书两用，既增长了知识，又提高了英语，算是一举两得吧。

最后我想感谢两位译者请我作序，让我有了先睹为快的机会。也感谢湖北少儿出版社为全中国的中小学生们献上的这份大礼。

祝你们阅读愉快！

陈乃芳

目录

1

走进树林

Into the Woods

　　杰克离开小路,走进树林。晚霞给树木披上了金装。

　　"快到这儿来!"安妮喊道。

　　她正站在一棵高大的橡树下,指着一架绳梯说:"瞧!"

"救命呀！大怪物！"安妮大喊道。

"啊，没错，"杰克说，"宾夕法尼亚州的蛙溪湾有一只真正的怪物。"

"快跑哇，杰克！"安妮一边叫着，一边顺着小路跑走了。

噢，真受不了！

跟七岁的妹妹耗时间尽遇到这种事儿。

安妮喜欢假想的东西，可是杰克已经八岁半了，他喜欢真实的事情。

"当心，杰克！怪物来了！咱俩看谁跑得快吧！"

"不，谢谢！"杰克说。

安妮一个人跑进了树林里。

杰克看看天空，太阳快要落山了。

"喂，安妮！该回家了！"

可是安妮不见了。

杰克等着。

没有安妮的影子。

"安妮！"杰克又喊了一遍。

"杰克！杰克！快过来！"

恐龙谷历险记

Dinosaurs
Before
Dark

杰克哼了一声，说："但愿这次是真的。"

杰克离开小路，走进树林。晚霞给树木披上了金装。

"快到这儿来！"安妮喊道。

她正站在一棵高大的橡树下，指着一架绳梯说："瞧！"

这可是杰克见过的最长的绳梯。

"哇！"他低声惊叹。

那梯子直达橡树的顶端。

而树的顶端居然有一间树屋，隐蔽在两个树杈之间。

"这肯定是世界上最高的树屋了！"安妮说。

"会是谁盖的呢？"杰克问，"我以前没在这儿看见过。"

"不知道，但是我要上去！"安妮说。

"不行，我们不知道这房子是谁的。"杰克说。

"就一小会儿！"安妮说着，开始沿着梯子往上爬。

"安妮，下来！"

可安妮继续往上爬。

杰克叹了口气，"安妮，天都快黑了，我们该回家了。"

安妮已经钻进树屋，不见人影了。

"安——妮！"

神奇树屋
MAGIC TREE HOUSE

　　杰克等了一会儿。他正准备再喊的时候,安妮的头从树屋的窗户探了出来。

　　"好多书呀!"她大叫道。

　　"什么?"

　　"这屋里堆满了书!"

　　噢,天哪!书可是杰克的至爱。

　　他把眼镜扶了扶,抓住绳梯的扶手开始向上爬。

怪物

The Monster

　　一个庞然大物正从树顶滑翔而过！脑袋后面有一个长长的、古怪的、鸡冠一样的东西，嘴巴又细又尖。还有两只巨大的蝙蝠状的翅膀！

　　那是一只真的、活的无齿翼龙！

杰克从树屋地板上的洞口爬了进去。

哇！屋子里堆满了书，到处都是。有很旧的、封面上积满了灰尘的书，也有封皮又光又亮的新书。

"你瞧，从这儿可以望到很远，很远！"安妮说。她正从树屋的窗户往外看。

杰克跟她一起向窗外望去。窗下是其他树的树顶；远处是蛙溪湾图书馆、小学、还有公园。

安妮指着另一个方向说："那是我们的房子。"

没错。那正是他们的白色木屋和绿色的门廊。隔壁趴着邻居家的黑狗——亨利。它看起来很小。

"喂，亨利！"安妮喊着。

"嘘！"杰克说，"我们不应该上到这儿来的。"

杰克又很快地环视了一下树屋。

"这些书到底是谁的呢？"他发现很多书的书签都突显出来。

"我喜欢这本书！"安妮说着举起一本封面上印着城堡的书。

"这儿有一本关于宾夕法尼亚的书。"杰克说。他翻到夹

有书签的那一页。

"嘿！这儿有一幅咱们蛙溪湾的插图呢！画的就是这片树林！"

"哎！这本书你肯定喜欢！"安妮说。她拿起一本关于恐龙的书，里面伸出一张蓝色丝质书签。

"让我看看。"杰克放下背包，从安妮手中一把抓过那本书。

"你看那本好了，我看这本关于城堡的书！"安妮说。

"不行，我们最好别看，"杰克说，"我们还不知道这些书是谁的呢。"

但是，尽管这么说，杰克还是翻开了那本关于恐龙的书，翻到有书签的那一页。

他看到一幅远古飞龙的画。那是一只无齿翼龙。

他抚摸着那巨大的蝙蝠状的翅膀。

"哇！"杰克低声自语，"真希望我能见到一只真正的无齿翼龙。"

杰克仔细研究着画里那只模样奇特、展翅翱翔的动物。

"哎呀！"安妮尖叫起来。

"怎么了？"杰克问。

"一个怪物！"安妮指着树屋的窗外叫喊着。

"别假装了，安妮！"杰克说。

"我没有假装，是真的！"安妮辩解道。

杰克向窗外望去。

一个庞然大物正从树顶滑翔而过！脑袋后面有一个长长的、古怪的、鸡冠一样的东西，嘴巴又细又尖。还有两只巨大的蝙蝠状的翅膀！

那是一只真的、活的无齿翼龙！

那怪物在空中拐了一个弯，笔直地向树屋飞来，看上去就像一架滑翔机！

风刮了起来。

树叶抖动着。

突然间，那怪物又骤然向上，直入云霄。杰克为了看清楚，差一点儿从窗口摔了出去。

风刮得更大了，发出呼呼的声响。

树屋开始旋转。

"怎么回事儿？"杰克喊道。

"快下来！"安妮尖叫着。

她把杰克从窗口拽了回来。

树屋继续旋转,越来越快。

杰克闭上眼睛,抓紧了安妮。

然后,一切都静止下来。

完全静止。

杰克睁开眼睛,阳光从树屋的窗户斜射进来。

安妮,那些书,还有他的背包都在。

树屋还是高高地挂在橡树顶上。

但已不是原来的那棵橡树了。

3 这是在哪儿?

Where Is Here?

不,不可能。他和安妮不可能降落到六千五百万年前。

"杰克,"安妮说,"那只无齿翼龙很友好。"

杰克向窗外望去。

他看看书上的那幅画。

他又回头看窗外。

外面的世界跟那幅画中的世界一模一样。

无齿翼龙正掠空而过。地面上覆盖着羊齿植物和高高的青草。一条蜿蜒的小溪，一座平缓的小山，还有远处的火山群，一切都不差分毫。

"我们，我们这是在哪儿呀？"杰克结结巴巴地说。

无齿翼龙滑行到他们所在的那棵树的底部，缓缓地停下来，一动不动。

"这到底是怎么回事儿啊？"安妮问。她看着杰克，杰克也看着她。

"我不知道，"杰克说，"我刚才在看书上的那幅插图——"

"接着，你说了，'哇，真希望我能看到一只真正的无齿翼龙。'"安妮补充道。

"是。然后我们就看到了一只，就在蛙溪湾的树林里。"杰克说。

"是呀！然后风就呼呼地刮，树屋就开始转！"安妮说。

"然后我们就降落在这儿！"杰克说。

"然后我们就降落在这儿！"安妮重复着。

"这就意味着……"杰克说。

"这就意味着……什么呢？"安妮问。

"没什么，"杰克摇摇头，"所有这一切都不可能是真的。"

安妮又朝窗外看去，"可是，这个怪物是真的呀，千真万确的呀！"

杰克和安妮一起望着窗外。无齿翼龙正在橡树底下站着。巨大的翅膀向两侧展开，就像一个卫士。

"你好！"安妮喊道。

"嘘！"杰克说，"我们不应该来这儿的。"

"可是，这是哪儿？"安妮问。

"我也不知道！"杰克说。

"你好！"安妮再次跟那只怪物打招呼。

无齿翼龙抬起头看着他俩。

"这是什么地方呀？"安妮向下喊道。

"你疯了吗？它不会说话，"杰克说，"不过这本书应该能告诉我们答案。"

杰克低头看书,无齿翼龙插图下面有两行文字:

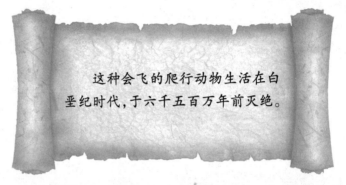

这种会飞的爬行动物生活在白垩纪时代,于六千五百万年前灭绝。

不,不可能。他和安妮不可能降落到六千五百万年前。

"杰克,"安妮说,"那只无齿翼龙很友好。"

"友好?"

"是,我看得出来,咱们下去跟它说说话吧。"

"跟它说话?"

安妮开始下绳梯。

"嘿!"杰克大叫。

可是安妮继续往下爬。

"你疯了?"杰克大喊。

安妮已经下到地面上,她勇敢地向那只远古动物走去。

亨利

Henry

那家伙盯着杰克,眼光明亮,眼神警觉。

"它很温柔,杰克,"安妮说,"它好像小狗亨利。"

杰克哼了一声,"它不是狗,安妮。"

安妮伸出手去摸那个庞然大物时,杰克倒吸了一口冷气。

天哪!天哪!她总是想跟动物交朋友,可这次也太玄乎了。

"别离它太近,安妮!"杰克大叫。

安妮碰了碰无齿翼龙的冠,又摸摸它的脖子。她在跟它说话呢。

她到底在说什么呢?

杰克深吸一口气。好吧,我也下去好了。这样能更好地观察那只动物,做点笔记什么的,像科学家一样。

杰克开始下绳梯。

落地后,杰克发现自己离那只动物只有几英尺远。

那家伙盯着杰克,眼光明亮,眼神警觉。

神奇树屋

MAGIC TREE HOUSE

"它很温柔,杰克,"安妮说,"它好像小狗亨利。"

杰克哼了一声,"它不是狗,安妮。"

"摸摸它,杰克!"安妮说。

杰克没有挪步。

"别犹豫了,杰克,就摸一下吧。"

杰克朝前挪了一步,伸出一只胳膊,非常小心地摸了摸那只怪物的脖子。

啊,有趣。一层薄薄的绒毛覆盖着无齿翼龙的皮肤。

"软乎吧?"安妮问。

杰克把手伸进背包,掏出一支铅笔和一个笔记本,写道:

毛绒绒的皮肤

"你在干什么?"安妮问。

"做笔记,"杰克说,"我们可能是世界上看到真的、活生

24

生的无齿翼龙的第一人呢。"

杰克又抬头看着无齿翼龙。这家伙的头顶上有个骨质硬冠，比杰克的胳膊还要粗。

"不知道它有多聪明呢！"杰克说。

"一定非常聪明！"安妮说。

"别自以为是，"杰克回答，"它的脑瓜也许比一颗豆儿大不了多少。"

"不，它肯定很聪明，我感觉得到，"安妮说，"我要叫它亨利。"

杰克在笔记本上写道：

小脑瓜

恐龙谷历险记
Dinosaurs
Before
Dark

他又看了看那个庞然大物，"说不定这是一个生物突变体。"

那家伙歪了歪脑袋。

安妮笑了，"它不是突变体，杰克。"

"那你说它在这儿干什么？这到底是什么地方？"

安妮将身体靠近无齿翼龙。

"你知道我们在哪儿吗，亨利？"她柔声地问。

那动物把目光定在安妮身上，长长的嘴巴一开一合，像一把大剪刀。

"你是在跟我说话吗，亨利？"安妮又问。

"算了吧，安妮。"杰克在笔记本上写道：

嘴巴像剪刀

"我们是不是来到了一个很久以前的年代，亨利？"安妮

继续问，"这儿是一个很久以前的地方吗？

突然她倒吸一口冷气，喊道："杰克！"

杰克抬起头。

安妮指着那座小山，山顶上正站着一只巨大的恐龙！

草丛里的金子

Gold in the Grass

　　杰克跟在安妮后面,他看见一个什么东西在高高的草丛里闪闪发光。他伸手把它拾了起来。

　　一枚勋章,一枚金子做的勋章。

恐龙谷历险记
*Dinosaurs
Before
Dark*

　　"快跑！快跑！"杰克喊道。他把笔记本扔进背包,将安妮推向绳梯。

　　"再见,亨利！"安妮说。

　　"快！"杰克一边催促,一边使劲儿推安妮。

　　"别再催了！"安妮抱怨道。她开始上梯子,杰克慌张地跟在后面。

　　他们跌跌撞撞地爬进树屋。

　　两人一边喘气,一边盯着窗外的那只恐龙。恐龙站在山顶上,吃着一棵树上的花朵。

　　"噢,天哪！"杰克小声嘀咕,"我们真的是回到了很久很久以前！"

　　那恐龙看起来像一头巨大的犀牛,只不过它有三只角而不是一只角。两只长角长在眼睛的上方,另一只长在鼻子上。脑袋后面还有一个盾形的东西。

　　"三角恐龙！"杰克说。

　　"它吃人吗？"安妮小声问道。

　　"我得查查书！"杰克抓起那本有关恐龙的书,飞快地翻着。

31

"你看！"他指着一张三角恐龙图片，读着说明：

三角恐龙生活在白垩纪末期，以植物为生，体重超过 12,000 磅。

杰克把书使劲合上，"它只吃植物，不吃肉。"

"那咱们去看看它！"安妮说。

"你疯了？"杰克说。

"难道你不想在笔记本里记下三角恐龙吗？"安妮问道，"我们没准儿是世界上看到真的、活的三角恐龙的第一人呢。"

杰克叹了口气。安妮说得对。

"咱们走吧！"他说。

他把那本关于恐龙的书塞进背包，将背包往肩上一甩，开始往绳梯下走。

下到一半，杰克停了下来。

恐龙谷历险记
Dinosaurs
Before
Dark

他对安妮喊道："你得保证这回你不去摸它。"

"我保证。"

"还得保证你不会去亲它。"

"我保证。"

"还得保证你不会跟它说话。"

"我保证。"

"还得保证你……"

"行了！行了！"安妮不耐烦了。

杰克继续往下爬。

安妮紧跟着。

他们跨下绳梯时，无齿翼龙友好地看了他们一眼。

安妮向它飞了个吻，高兴地说："我们马上就回来，亨利。"

"嘘！"杰克制止了她。他在前面领路，慢慢地、小心地穿过那片羊齿植物。

到达山脚后，杰克跪在一丛茂密的灌木后面。

安妮在他旁边跪下，开始嘟哝。

"嘘！"杰克把食指放在嘴唇前。

安妮做了个鬼脸。

杰克偷偷地窥视那只三角恐龙。

那家伙个头儿魁梧，比一辆卡车还大，正在吃一棵玉兰树上的花。

杰克悄悄地从背包里拿出笔记本，写道：

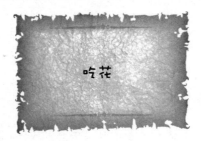

吃花

安妮推了他一下。

杰克没有理睬她。他仔细观察三角龙，又写道：

吃得很慢

安妮使劲推了他一下。

杰克看着她。

安妮指着自己，用手指头在空气中比划着，然后指向恐龙。她笑了。

她是在逗乐吗？

她向杰克挥挥手。

杰克想去抓她。

可是她笑哈哈地跳开了，跌倒在草丛里，完全暴露在三角恐龙的视野里。

"回来！"杰克轻声地叫喊。

太晚了，大恐龙已经看到安妮了。它从山顶向下注视着安妮。半朵玉兰花还挂在嘴角。

"啊呀！"安妮叫了一声。

"回来！"杰克冲她喊道。

"它看起来很温顺，杰克。"

"温顺？当心它的角，安妮！"

"没事儿。它真的很温顺，杰克。"

温顺吗？

三角恐龙只是静静地注视着安妮，然后转身慢慢地走开了，走向山的那一边。

"再见！"安妮说。她转向杰克，"我说得没错儿吧？"

杰克嘟哝了一句什么，在笔记本上写道：

温顺

"来，咱们再到周围多看看！"安妮说。

杰克跟在安妮后面，他看见一个什么东西在高高的草丛里闪闪发光。他伸手把它拾了起来。

一枚勋章，一枚金子做的勋章。

勋章上刻着一个字母，一个别致的 M。

"噢，天哪！有人在我们之前就来过这里了！"杰克轻声说道。

6 恐龙山谷

Dinosaur Valley

到达山顶时,他累得上气不接下气。

山谷里布满了巢穴,用泥土做的大大的巢穴,里面全是小恐龙!

"安妮,你看这个!"杰克喊道,"看我发现了什么!"

安妮已经爬到了山顶。

她在忙着摘玉兰树上的花。

"安妮,快看!一枚勋章!"

可是安妮并没有注意杰克。她正注视山那边的什么东西。

"噢,哇!"她惊讶地说。

"安妮!"杰克喊道。

安妮握着玉兰花下山了!

"安妮,回来!"杰克高声喊着。

可是安妮已经不见了。

"看我怎么收拾你!"杰克咬牙切齿。

他把金质勋章放进牛仔裤的口袋里。

接着就听到安妮的尖叫。

"安妮?"

杰克又听到另外一个声音,一个低沉的吼声,好像低音喇叭似的。

"杰克!快来呀!"安妮叫喊着。

"安妮!"

杰克抓起背包就往山顶冲。

到达山顶时,他累得上气不接下气。

山谷里布满了巢穴,用泥土做的大大的巢穴,里面全是小恐龙!

安妮正蹲伏在一个巢穴旁,一只巨大的长着鸭嘴的恐龙就站在她身边!

"别慌!别动!"杰克喊着,他慢慢走下山坡,走近安妮。

巨大的恐龙耸立在安妮身边,挥舞着双臂,发出低音喇叭似的吼声。

杰克站住了。他不想走得太近。

他跪在地上说:"好了,你慢慢往我这边挪。"

安妮试着站起来。

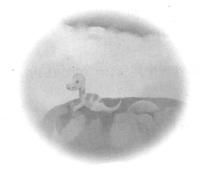

"别站起来,要爬行!"杰克吩咐。

安妮手里还攥着玉兰花,她向杰克爬去。

鸭嘴恐龙跟着她,继续低吼。

安妮吓呆了。

"继续爬!"杰克轻声鼓励。

安妮接着爬。

杰克慢慢往山下挪动,直到他与安妮仅一臂之隔。

他把手伸出去,抓住安妮的手。

他把安妮往自己身边拽。

"快蹲下,"他这样嘱咐。两人并排蹲着,杰克说,"快低头,假装咀嚼。"

"咀嚼?"

"对,书上说如果一条恶狗向你走来,你就得这样做。"

"可那鸭嘴家伙不是狗,杰克!"安妮说。

"你就咀嚼吧!"杰克命令道。

杰克和安妮都低下头,假装咀嚼。

很快那只恐龙安静下来。

杰克抬起头。

"我想它已经不再发疯了！"他说。

"谢谢你救了我，杰克！"安妮说。

"你得多动脑筋，"杰克说，"你不能径直往恐龙宝宝的巢穴里跑，那附近总会有恐龙妈妈在守候的。"

安妮站了起来。

"安妮！"

来不及了。

安妮向恐龙妈妈举起她的玉兰花。

"对不起，我让你担心你的宝宝了！"安妮说。

恐龙向安妮走近。它夺过安妮的花，还想再要。

"没有了！"安妮说。

恐龙发出一种可怜的低音喇叭似的吼声。

安妮指着山顶，说："那上面还有好多花呢，我再去给你摘几朵。"

安妮向山顶跑去。

恐龙摇摇摆摆地跟在她身后。

杰克抓紧时间观察那些恐龙宝宝，有些正在往外爬。

其他的妈妈在哪儿呢？

杰克拿出那本关于恐龙的书，飞快地翻着。

他找到一张鸭嘴恐龙的图片。图片下写着：

鸭嘴恐龙过着群居生活。一些妈妈守在小恐龙身边，其他的妈妈去猎取食物。

所以附近一定还有更多的恐龙妈妈。

"嘿！杰克！"安妮喊道。

杰克抬起头，看见安妮站在山顶上，正给那只大鸭嘴恐龙喂玉兰花呢！

"它也很温顺，杰克！"安妮说。

但是，突然间，鸭嘴恐龙又发出可怕的、低音喇叭似的吼声。安妮往地上一趴，开始假装咀嚼。

恐龙大步冲下山。

它看起来好像很慌张。

　　杰克把书往背包顶上一放,跑向安妮。

　　"真不明白它为什么跑开呢?"安妮说,"我们都快成为朋友了。"

　　杰克向四周一望,远处的一个怪物吓得他差点吐了。

　　一个巨大而丑陋的怪物正穿过山脚的平地。

　　它用两条大粗腿走路,两只小胳膊垂着,一条又长又粗的尾巴来回摆动。

　　它的头非常大,嘴巴张开,大得吓人。

　　尽管离得很远,杰克还是能清楚地看到它那长长的、闪着寒光的牙齿。

　　"霸王龙!"杰克轻声说。

7

各就各位，预备，跑！

Ready, Set, Go!

杰克深吸一口气。

各就各位！预备！跑！

他猛冲下山，一个箭步跳到背包旁，一把抓起背包和那本恐龙书。

"快跑,安妮!快跑!"杰克高声叫喊着,"快回树屋!"

他们一起冲下山,穿过高高的草丛,越过羊齿植物,从无齿翼龙身边跑过,终于来到绳梯下。

他们飞快地登上绳梯,转眼间就钻进了树屋。

安妮跳到窗户旁边。

"霸王龙已经走了!"她气喘吁吁地说。

杰克扶了扶眼镜,跟安妮一起往窗外看。

霸王龙正漫步离开。

突然那怪物又停下脚步,转过身来。

"把头低下!"杰克叫着。

俩人一起弯下腰。

过了好一会儿,他们抬起头,再向窗外偷看。

"警报解除!"杰克说。

"呀!"安妮轻轻松了口气。

"我们得离开这儿。"杰克说。

"你先前是许了个愿咱们才来到这儿的。"安妮提醒他。

"我希望我们能够回到蛙溪湾。"杰克再次许愿。

可是什么动静都没有。

"我希望……"

"等等,你先前许愿的时候是看着恐龙书中的一幅画的,记得吗?"

恐龙书。

"噢,坏了!"杰克叫起来,"我把书和背包都丢在山上了。我得回去拿。"

"算了吧!"安妮说。

"不行,"杰克说,"那书不是我们的。再说,我的笔记本和所有的笔记都在背包里。"

"那就赶快呀!"安妮说。

杰克急忙下了绳梯。

他跳到地面上。

他从无齿翼龙身边跑过,越过那片羊齿植物,穿过高高的草丛,往山顶跑去。

他从山顶往下看。

他的背包就在山谷的地上,上面还放着那本恐龙书。

可是,现在山谷里站满了鸭嘴恐龙,它们都在守卫自己的巢穴。

它们刚才都去哪儿了？是因为惧怕霸王龙的袭击才回到自己的巢穴吗？

杰克深吸一口气。

各就各位！预备！跑！

他猛冲下山，一个箭步跳到背包旁，一把抓起背包和那本恐龙书。

一个可怕的低音喇叭似的吼声突然响起。又一声！又一声！所有的鸭嘴恐龙都在向他吼叫。

杰克拔脚就跑。

他向山顶飞奔。

他开始下山了。

他收住脚。

霸王恐龙回来了！就站在杰克和树屋之间。

巨大的身影

A Giant Shadow

就在这时，一个巨大的影子将杰克罩住。他抬起头。

无齿翼龙正在他头顶滑行，庞大的身躯向着山顶滑落。

杰克跳到玉兰树后面。

他的心怦怦乱跳,使他几乎无法思考。

他窥视那头巨大的怪物。那个相貌狰狞的家伙正张着血盆大口,露出像牛排刀一样大的牙齿。

别慌。得想办法。

杰克看看下面的山谷。

很好。那些鸭嘴恐龙还在守护自己的巢穴。

杰克回头看霸王龙。

很好。这个蠢家伙看起来还不知道自己在哪儿。

别慌。想办法,想办法。也许恐龙书上会有什么高招。

杰克翻开恐龙书,找到有关霸王龙的介绍:

霸王龙是有史以来陆地上最大的肉食动物。

如果它至今还活着,一口就能吃掉一个人。

好嘛！这书一点帮助都没有。

好吧,他不能躲到小山那边去,因为那样会让鸭嘴龙四散惊跑。

好吧,他也没法跑进树屋,因为霸王龙会跑得更快。

好吧,看来他只能等下去,等到那怪物离开。

杰克从树后偷看。

霸王龙离小山更近了。

突然一个什么东西在眼前一晃。安妮正在下绳梯!

难道她发疯了? 她想干什么?

杰克看着安妮跳下绳梯。

她径直往无齿翼龙走去。她在跟它讲话。她挥舞双臂,指指杰克,指指天空,又指了指树屋。

她肯定是疯了。

"走啊! 快回到树上去!"杰克喃喃自语,"走啊!"

突然,杰克听到一声咆哮。

霸王龙正朝着他的方向张望。

杰克匍在地面上。

霸王龙正朝着小山走来。

神奇树屋
MAGIC TREE HOUSE

杰克感到地面在摇晃。

他该逃跑吗？还是爬回恐龙山谷？还是爬上玉兰树？

就在这时，一个巨大的影子将杰克罩住。他抬起头。

无齿翼龙正在他头顶滑行，庞大的身躯向着山顶滑落。

它是为杰克而来的。

9 奇妙的飞行

The Amazing Ride

他高兴地喊着，笑着。

他真不敢相信，他竟然骑在一只远古飞龙的背上飞行！

恐龙谷历险记

Dinosaurs
Before
Dark

　　无齿翼龙缓缓降落到地面。

　　它用明亮而警惕的眼光注视着杰克。

　　杰克该怎么做呢？爬到它的背上去吗？"可我太沉了！"杰克寻思。

　　别想了，就这么办吧。

　　杰克看看那只霸王龙。

　　它正在上山，巨大的牙齿在阳光下闪着凛凛寒光。

　　好了，别想了，就这么着吧！

　　杰克把书放进背包，小心翼翼地爬到无齿翼龙背上。

　　他紧紧抱着无齿翼龙。

　　无齿翼龙向前迈步，张开翅膀，拔地而起。

　　他们忽左忽右，时高时低。

　　杰克几乎要掉下来。

　　无齿翼龙稳住方向，飞向天空。

　　杰克俯视下方。霸王龙在吧哒吧哒地吃着空气，眼巴巴地望着他。

　　无齿翼龙驮着杰克飞走了。

　　它翱翔在山顶的上空。

63

　　它在山谷的上方盘旋,在恐龙宝宝的巢穴和巨大的鸭嘴恐龙头顶盘旋。

　　它翱翔在平原的上空——从那些正在茂密的草丛中吃草的三角恐龙的头顶掠过。

　　太爽了! 太神奇了!

　　杰克感到自己就像一只小鸟,像羽毛一样轻。

　　风儿吹拂着他的头发,空气又甜美又清新。

　　他高兴地喊着,笑着。

　　他真不敢相信,他竟然骑在一只远古飞龙的背上飞行!

　　无齿翼龙飞过小溪,飞过那片羊齿植物和灌木丛。

　　它带着杰克降落在橡树底下。

　　等无齿翼龙停稳了,杰克才从它的背上溜下来,落到地面上。

　　无齿翼龙再次腾空而起。

　　"再见,亨利!"杰克轻声地说。

　　"你没事儿吧?"安妮从树屋里喊道。

　　杰克扶了扶眼镜,久久地望着那只无齿翼龙。

　　"杰克,你没事儿吧?"安妮又叫道。

杰克抬头望着安妮,笑了。

"谢谢你救了我,"他说,"刚才真太有趣了!"

"上来吧!"安妮说。

杰克努力想站起来,可是双腿发麻,不听使唤。

他觉得有点头晕。

"快!"安妮叫道,"它来了!"

杰克回头一看,霸王龙正向他冲来!

杰克箭一般地冲向绳梯,抓住两侧扶手往上爬。

"快!快!"安妮尖叫着。

杰克一头撞进树屋。

"它在向橡树走来!"安妮大叫。

突然间一个什么东西撞在橡树上。树屋像树叶一样颤抖。

杰克和安妮挤成一团钻进书堆里。

"赶紧许愿!"安妮嚷着。

"我们需要那本书!那本有蛙溪湾图片的书!"杰克说,"书在哪儿?"

他把一堆书推向一边。他得找出那本关于宾夕法尼亚的书。

在这儿！

他一把抓起书，急速地翻找蛙溪湾树林的图片。

找到了！杰克指着那幅画大叫：

"我希望我们能够回家！"

风开始呜呜地吹，一开始很轻柔。

"赶快呀！"杰克吼道。

风大起来了，开始呼啸。

树屋开始旋转。

它越转越快。

杰克闭上眼睛，紧紧抓住安妮。

然后一切归于静止。

完全静止。

10 天黑前回家

Home Before Dark

"我们回家了！"安妮轻声说。

金色的晚霞照射着树林。太阳就要落山了。

自从他们离开,时间并没有流逝。

小鸟开始唱歌。

杰克睁开双眼。他的手仍然指着那幅蛙溪湾树林的图片。

他从树屋的窗户向外窥视。外面的景色跟他离开时一模一样。

"我们回家了！"安妮轻声说。

金色的晚霞照射着树林。太阳就要落山了。

自从他们离开，时间并没有流逝。

"杰——克！安——妮！"远远地传来呼唤。

"是妈妈！"安妮指着远处说道。

杰克也看到了远处的妈妈，她正站在家门口，显得很小。

"安——妮！杰——克！"妈妈还在呼唤。

安妮把脑袋伸出窗外回答："来了！"

杰克仍然感到头晕。他盯着安妮。

"到底发生了什么事？"他问。

"我们在这间神奇树屋里做了一次旅行。"安妮简简单单地回答。

"可是时间还是我们离开时的时间呀！"杰克说。

安妮耸耸肩。

"树屋怎么能把我们带到那么遥远、那么古老的地方呢？"杰克不解地追问。

"你就是看着一本书，说你希望我们能到那儿去，"安妮回答，"然后神奇树屋就把我们带到那儿去了呗。"

"可是怎么带的呢？"杰克问，"是谁建的这间神奇树屋？又是谁把这些书放在这儿的？"

"我猜想是一个会魔法的人。"安妮说。

一个会魔法的人？

"噢，想起来了，"杰克说，"我差点把这个给忘了。"他把手伸进口袋，掏出那枚金质勋章。"不知谁把这枚勋章落在那儿了……我是说恐龙的家园。你看，这上面还刻着一个字母 M。"

安妮眼珠一转，问："你觉得 M 是代表会魔法的人吗？"

"我不知道，"杰克说，"我只知道在我们之前就有人到过那地方。"

"杰——克！安——妮！"远处的呼唤再次响起。

安妮把脑袋探出窗外，高声回答："来了！"

杰克把金质勋章放回口袋里。

他把那本恐龙书从背包里拿出来，和其他的书放在一起。

他和安妮最后看了一眼树屋。

"再见了，树屋！"安妮轻声说。

杰克把背包往肩上一甩，用手指指绳梯。

安妮开始往下爬，杰克跟着。

一眨眼他们就到了地面，两人向树林外走去。

"没有人会相信我们的故事！"杰克说。

"所以咱们就别告诉任何人！"安妮回答。

"爸爸是不会相信的！"杰克说。

"他会说那是做梦！"安妮附和。

"妈妈是不会相信的！"杰克说。

"她会说那是想象。"安妮表示同意。

"老师也不会相信。"杰克说。

"她会说你疯了！"安妮点头。

"我们最好不要告诉任何人！"杰克说。

"对啊，我就是这么说的！"安妮再次点头。

杰克叹了口气，"我觉得我开始不相信自己了。"

他们离开树林，走上回家的路。

　　他们走过街道两旁的房屋，回到恐龙时代的旅行越来越像是做了一场梦。

　　只有这个世界、这个时间才是真实的。

　　杰克把手伸进口袋，紧握着那枚金质勋章。

　　他摸着勋章上镌刻的字母 M，手指微微地被刺痛。

　　杰克笑了。他突然感到非常高兴。

　　他不能解释今天到底发生了什么。但他确信，他们在神奇树屋里的旅行是真的。

　　绝对是真的。

　　"明天，"杰克柔声地说，"我们再回到这片树林。"

　　"当然！"安妮说。

　　"我们还要爬进那间树屋！"杰克说。

　　"当然！"安妮说。

　　"我们要看看下一步还会发生什么？"杰克说。

　　"当然，"安妮说，"来，看谁跑得快！"

　　兄妹俩一起向家门口跑去。

恐龙谷历险记

●恐龙在地球上存在了一亿五千多万年。杰克和安妮所到的白垩纪晚期是恐龙就要灭绝的时候。霸王龙、三角龙、无齿翼龙、鸭嘴龙都是最后的恐龙。

●很多恐龙都有母性，连霸王龙都会筑巢、下蛋、养育幼崽。像鸭嘴龙这样的食草恐龙有很强的社会性，母亲们会聚在一起共同养育和保护恐龙宝宝。

●翼龙是恐龙时代天空的霸主，今天的天空已经被鸟类占据。鸟类并不是翼龙的后代。研究表明，今天鸟类的祖先很可能是某种陆上的小恐龙。

●有的专家认为恐龙的灭绝和当时的气候变冷以及频繁的火山喷发有关，所以白垩纪时，到处是火山频发的景象。

恐龙谷历险记
DINOSAURS BEFORE DARK

恐龙谷历险记

DINOSAURS BEFORE DARK

CONTENTS

1

Into the Woods

"Help! A monster!" said Annie.

"Yeah, sure," said Jack. "A real monster in Frog Creek, Pennsylvania."

"Run, Jack!" said Annie. She ran up the road.

Oh, brother.

This is what he got for spending time with his seven-year-old sister.

Annie loved pretend stuff. But Jack was eight and a half. He liked *real* things.

"Watch out, Jack! The monster's coming! Race you!"

"No, thanks," said Jack.

Annie raced alone into the woods.

Jack looked at the sky. The sun was about to set.

"Come on, Annie! It's time to go home!"

But Annie had disappeared.

Jack waited.

No Annie.

"Annie!" he shouted again.

"Jack! Jack! Come here!"

Jack groaned. "This better be good," he said.

Jack left the road and headed into the woods. The trees
were lit with a golden late afternoon light.

"Come here!" called Annie.

There she was. Standing under a tall oak tree. "Look,"
she said. She was pointing at a rope ladder.

The longest rope ladder Jack had ever seen.

"Wow," he whispered.

The ladder went all the way up to the top of the tree.

There—at the top—was a tree house. It was tucked
between two branches.

"That must be the highest tree house in the world,"
said Annie.

"Who built it ?" asked Jack. "I've never seen it before."

"I don't know. But I'm going up," said Annie.

"No. We don't know who it belongs to," said Jack.

"Just for a teeny minute,"said Annie. She started up the ladder.

"Annie, come back!"

She kept climbing.

Jack sighed. "Annie, it's almost dark. We have to go home."

Annie disappeared inside the tree house.

"An-nie!"

Jack waited a moment. He was about to call again when Annie poked her head out of the tree house window.

"Books!" she shouted.

"What?"

"It's filled with books!"

Oh, man! Jack loved books.

He pushed his glasses into place. He gripped the sides of the rope ladder, and up he went.

The Monster

Jack crawled through a hole in the tree house floor.

Wow. The tree house *was* filled with books. Books everywhere. Very old books with dusty covers. New books with shiny, bright covers.

"Look. You can see far, far away," said Annie. She was peering out the tree house window.

Jack looked out the window with her. Down below were the tops of the other trees. In the distance he saw the Frog Creek library. The elementary school. The park.

Annie pointed in the other direction.

"There's our house," she said.

Sure enough. There was their white wooden house with the green porch. Next door was their neighbor's black dog, Henry. He looked very tiny.

"Hi, Henry!" shouted Annie.

"Shush!" said Jack. "We're not supposed to be up

here."

He glanced around the tree house again.

"I wonder who owns all these books," he said. He noticed bookmarks were sticking out of many of them.

"I like this one," said Annie. She held up a book with a castle on the cover.

"Here's a book about Pennsylvania," said Jack. He turned to the page with the bookmark.

"Hey, there's a picture of Frog Creek in here," said Jack. "It's a picture of *these* woods!"

"Oh, here's a book for you," said Annie. She held up a book about dinosaurs. A blue silk bookmark was sticking out of it.

"Let me see it." Jack set down his backpack and grabbed the book from her.

"You look at that one, and I'll look at the one about

castles，" said Annie.

"No，We better not，" said Jack. "We don't know who these books belong to."

But even as he said this，Jack opened the dinosaur book to where the bookmark was. He couldn't help himself.

He turned to a picture of an ancient flying reptile. A Pteranodon.

He touched the huge bat-like wings.

"Wow，" whispered Jack. "I wish I could see a Pteranodon for real."

Jack studied the picture of the odd-looking creature soaring through the sky.

"Ahhh!" screamed Annie.

"What？" said Jack.

"A monster!" Annie cried. She pointed to the tree house window.

神奇 树 屋

MAGIC TREE HOUSE

"Stop pretending, Annie," said Jack.

"No, really!" said Annie.

Jack looked out the window.

A giant creature was gliding above the treetops! He had a long, weird crest on the back of his head. A skinny beak. And huge bat-like wings!

It was a real live Pteranodon!

恐龙谷历险记
Dinosaurs
Before
Dark

The creature curved through the sky. He was coming

straight toward the tree house. He looked like a glider plane!

The wind began to blow.

The leaves trembled.

Suddenly the creature soared up. High into the sky.

Jack nearly fell out the window trying to see it.

The wind picked up. It was whistling now.

The tree house started to spin.

"What's happening?" cried Jack.

"Get down!" shouted Annie.

She pulled him back from the window.

The tree house was spinning. Faster and faster.

Jack squeezed his eyes shut. He held on to Annie.

Then everything was still.

Absolutely still.

Jack opened his eyes. Sunlight slanted through the

window.

There was Annie. The books. His backpack.

The tree house was still high up in an oak tree.

But it wasn't the *same* oak tree.

Where Is Here?

Jack looked out the window.

He looked down at the picture in the book.

He looked back out the window.

The world outside and the world in the picture—they were exactly the same.

The Pteranodon was soaring through the sky. The ground was covered with ferns and tall grass. There was a winding stream. A sloping hill. And volcanoes in the distance.

"Wh—where are we?" stammered Jack.

The Pteranodon glided down to the base of their tree. The creature

coasted to a stop. And stood very still.

"What happened to us?" said Annie. She looked at Jack. He looked at her.

"I don't know," said Jack. "I was looking at the picture in the book—"

"And you said, 'Wow, I wish I could see a Pteranodon for real,'" said Annie.

"Yeah. And then we saw one. In the Frog Creek woods", said Jack.

"Yeah. And then the wind got loud. And the tree house started spinning," said Annie.

"And we landed here," said Jack.

"And we landed here," said Annie.

"So that means..." said Jack.

"So that means... what?" said Annie.

"Nothing," said Jack. He shook his head. "None of

this can be real."

Annie looked out the window again. "But *he's* real," she said. "He's *very* real."

Jack looked out the window with her. The Pteranodon was standing at the base of the oak tree. Like a guard. His giant wings were spread out on either side of him.

"Hi!" Annie shouted.

"Shush!" said Jack."we're not supposed to be here."

"But where is *here?*" said Annie.

"I don't know," said Jack.

"Hi!" Annie called again to the creature.

The Pteranodon looked up at them.

"Where is *here?*" Annie called down.

"You're nuts. He can't talk," said Jack. "But maybe the book can tell us."

Jack looked down at the book. He read the words under

the picture:

This flying reptile lived in the Cretaceous period. It vanished 65 million years ago.

No. Impossible. They couldn't have landed in a time 65 million years ago.

"Jack," said Annie. "He's nice."

"Nice?"

"Yeah, I can tell. Let's go down and talk to him."

"Talk to him?"

Annie started down the rope ladder.

"Hey!" shouted Jack.

But Annie kept going.

"Are you crazy?" Jack called.

Annie dropped to the ground. She stepped boldly up to the ancient creature.

Henry

恐龙谷历险记

Dinosaurs
Before
Dark

Jack gasped as Annie held out her hand.

Oh, brother. She was always trying to make friends
with animals. But this was going too far.

"Don't get too close to him, Annie!" Jack shouted.

But Annie touched the Pteranodon's crest. She stroked
his neck. She was talking to him.

What in the world was she saying?

Jack took a deep breath. Okay. He would go down too.
It would be good to examine the creature. Take notes. Like
a scientist.

Jack started down the rope ladder.

When he got to the ground, Jack was only a few feet
away from the creature.

The creature stared at Jack. His eyes were bright and
alert.

"He's soft, Jack," said Annie. "He feels like Henry."

•   101   •

Jack snorted. "He's no dog, Annie."

"Feel him, Jack," said Annie.

Jack didn't move.

"Don't think, Jack. Just do it."

Jack stepped forward. He put out his arm. Very cautiously. He brushed his hand down the creature's neck.

· Interesting. A thin layer of fuzz covered the Pteranodon's skin.

"Soft, huh?" said Annie.

Jack reached into his backpack and pulled out a pencil and a notebook. He wrote:

fuzzy skin

"What are you doing?" asked Annie.

"Taking notes," said Jack. "We're probably the first people in the whole world to ever see a real live Pteranodon."

Jack looked at the Pteranodon again. The creature had a bony crest on top of his head. The crest was longer than Jack's arm.

"I wonder how smart he is," Jack said.

"*Very* smart," said Annie.

"Don't count on it," said Jack. "His brain's probably no bigger than a bean."

"No, he's very smart. I can feel it," said Annie. "I'm goint to call him Henry."

Jack wrote in his notebook:

small brain?

Jack looked at the creature again. "Maybe he's a mutant," he said.

The creature tilted his head.

Annie laughed. "He's no mutant, Jack."

"Well, what's he doing here then? Where is this place?" said Jack.

Annie leaned close to the Pteranodon.

"Do you know where we are, Henry?" she asked softly.

The creature fixed his eyes on Annie. His long jaws were opening and closing. Like a giant pair of scissors.

"Are you trying to talk to me, Henry?" asked Annie.

"Forget it, Annie." Jack wrote in his notebook:

mouth like scissors?

"Did we come to a time long ago, Henry?" asked Annie. "Is this a place from long ago?" Suddenly she gasped. "Jack!"

He looked up.

Annie was pointing toward the hill. On top stood a huge dinosaur!

Gold in the Grass

神奇树屋

MAGIC TREE HOUSE

"Go! *Go!*" said Jack. He threw his notebook into his pack. He pushed Annie toward the rope ladder.

"Bye, Henry!" she siad.

"Go!" said Jack. He gave Annie a big push.

"Quit it!" she said. But she started up the ladder. Jack scrambled after her.

They tumbled into the tree house.

They were panting as they looked out the window at the dinosaur. He was standing on the hilltop. Eating flowers off a tree.

"Oh, man," whispered Jack. "We *are* in a time long ago!"

The dinosaur looked like a huge rhinoceros. Only he had three horns instead of one. Two long ones above his eyes and one on his nose. He had a big shield-like thing behind his head.

· 108 ·

恐龙谷历险记

Dinosaurs
Before
Dark

"Triceratops!" said Jack.

"Does he eat people?" whispered Annie.

"I'll look it up." Jack grabbed the dinosaur book. He flipped through the pages.

"There!" he said. He pointed to a picture of a Triceratops. He read the caption:

> **The Triceratops lived in the late Cretaceous period. This plant-eating dinosaur weighed over 12,000 pounds.**

Jack slammed the book shut. "Just plants. No meat."

"Let's go see him," said Annie.

"Are you nuts?" said Jack.

"Don't you want to take notes about him?" asked Annie.

"We're probably the first people in the whole world to ever see a real live Triceratops."

Jack sighed. She was right.

"Let's go," he said.

He shoved the dinosaur book into his pack. He slung it over his shoulder and started down the ladder.

On the way down, Jack stopped.

He called up to Annie, "Just promise you won't pet him."

"I promise."

"Promise you won't kiss him."

"I promise."

"Promise you won't talk to him."

"I promise."

"Promise you won't—"

"Go! Go!" she siad.

Jack went.

Annie followed.

When they stepped off the ladder, the Pteranodon gave them a kind look.

Annie blew a kiss at him. "Be back soon, Henry," she said cheerfully.

"Shush!" said Jack. And he led the way through the ferns. Slowly and carefully.

When he reached the bottom of the hill, he kneeled behind a fat bush.

Annie knelt beside him and started to speak.

"Shush!" Jack put his finger to his lips.

Annie made a face.

Jack peeked out at the Triceratops.

The dinosaur was incredibly big. Bigger than a truck. He was eating the flowers off a magnolia tree.

Jack slipped his notebook out of his pack. He wrote:

eats flowers

Annie nudged him.

Jack ignored her. He studied the Triceratops again. He

wrote:

eats slowly

Annie nudged him hard.

Jack looked at her.

Annie pointed to herself.   She walked her fingers

恐龙谷历险记
Dinosaurs
Before
Dark

through the air. She pointed to the dinosaur. She smiled.

Was she teasing?

She waved at Jack.

Jack started to grab her.

She laughed and jumped away. She fell into the grass. In full view of the Triceratops!

"Get back!" whispered Jack.

Too late. The big dinosaur had spotted Annie. He gazed down at her from the hilltop. Half of a magnolia flower was sticking out of his mouth.

"Oops," said Annie.

"Get back!" Jack shouted at her.

"He looks nice, Jack."

"Nice? Watch out for his horns, Annie!"

"No. He's nice, Jack."

Nice?

But the Triceratops just gazed calmly down at Annie.
Then he turned and loped away. Down the side of the hill.

"Bye!" said Annie. She turned back to Jack. "See?"

Jack grunted. But he wrote in his notebook.

nice

"Come on. Let's look around some more," said Annie.

As Jack started after Annie, he saw something glittering
in the tall grass. He reached out and picked it up.

A medallion. A gold medallion.

A letter was engraved on the medallion. A fancy M.

"Oh, man. Someone came here before us," Jack said
softly.

Dinosaur Valley

"Annie, look at this!" Jack called. "Look what I found!"

Annie had gone up to the hilltop.

She was busy picking a flower from the magnolia tree.

"Annie, look! A medallion!"

But Annie wasn't paying attention to Jack. She was staring at something on the other side of the hill.

"Oh, wow!" she said.

"Annie!"

Clutching her magnolia flower, she took off down the hill.

"Annie, come back!" Jack shouted.

But Annie had disappeared.

"I'm goint to kill her," Jack muttered.

He stuffed the gold medallion into his jeans pocket.

Then he heard Annie shriek.

恐龙谷历险记
Dinosaurs
Before
Dark

"Annie?"

Jack heard another sound as well. A deep, bellowing sound. Like a tuba.

"Jack! Come here!" Annie called.

"Annie!"

Jack grabbed his backpack and raced up the hill.

When he got to the top, he gasped.

The valley below was filled with nests. Big nests made out of mud. And the nests were filled with tiny dinosaurs!

Annie was crouching next to one of the nests. And standing over her was a gigantic duck-billed dinosaur!

"Don't panic. Don't move," said Jack. He stepped slowly down the hill toward Annie.

The huge dinosaur was towering above Annie. Waving her arms. Making her tuba sound.

Jack stopped. He didn't want to get too close.

He knelt on the ground. "Okay. Move toward me. Slowly," he said.

Annie started to stand up.

"Don't stand. Crawl," said Jack.

Clutching her flower, Annie crawled toward Jack.

The duck-billed dinosaur followed her. Still bellowing.

Annie froze.

"Keep going," Jack said softly.

Annie started crawling again.

Jack inched farther down the hill. Until he was just an arm's distance from Annie.

He reached out—and grabbed her hand.

He pulled Annie toward him.

"Stay down," he said. He crouched next to her. "Bow your head. Pretend to chew."

"Chew?"

"Yes. I read that's what you do if a mean dog comes at you."

"She's no dog, Jack," said Annie.

"Just chew," said Jack.

Jack and Annie both bowed their heads. And pretended to chew.

Soon the dinosaur grew quiet.

Jack raised his head.

"I don't think she's mad anymore," he said.

"Thanks, Jack, for saving me," said Annie.

"You have to use your brain," said Jack. "You can't just go running to a nest of babies. There's always a mother nearby."

Annie stood up.

"Annie!"

Too late.

Annie held out her magnolia flower to the dinosaur.

"I'm sorry I made you worry about your babies," she said.

The dinosaur moved closer to Annie. She grabbed the flower from her. She reached for another.

"No more," said Annie.

The dinosaur let out a sad tuba sound.

"But there are more flowers up there," Annie said. She pointed to the top of the hill. "I'll get you some."

Annie hurried up the hill.

The dinosaur waddled after her.

Jack quickly examined the babies. Some were crawling out of their nests.

Where were the other mothers?

Jack took out the dinosaur book. He flipped through the pages.

He found a picture of some duck-billed dinosaurs. He read the caption:

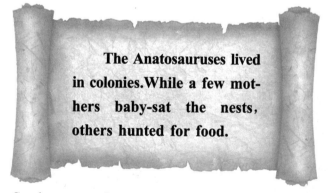

The Anatosauruses lived in colonies. While a few mothers baby-sat the nests, others hunted for food.

So there must be more mothers close by.

"Hey, Jack!" Annie called.

Jack looked up. Annie was at the top of the hill. Feeding magnolia flowers to the giant Anatosaurus!

"She's nice, too, Jack," Annie said.

But suddenly the Anatosaurus made her terrible tuba sound. Annie crouched down and started to chew.

The dinosaur barged down the hill.

She seemed afraid of something.

Jack put the book down on top of his pack. He hurried up to Annie.

"I wonder why she ran away," said Annie. "We were starting to be friends."

Jack looked around. What he saw in the distance almost made him throw up.

An enormous ugly monster was coming across the plain.

He was walking on two big legs. And swinging a long,

thick tail. And dangling two tiny arms.

He had a huge head. And his jaws were wide open.

Even from far away Jack could see his long, gleaming teeth.

"Tyrannosaurus rex!" whispered Jack.

Ready, Set, Go!

"Run, Annie! Run!" cried Jack. "To the tree house!"

They dashed down the hill together. Through the tall grass, through the ferns, past the Pteranodon, and right to the rope ladder.

They scrambled up. Seconds later they tumbled into the tree house.

Annie leaped to the window.

"He's going away!" she said, panting.

Jack pushed his glasses into place. He looked through the window with her.

The Tyrannosaurus was wandering off.

But then the monster stopped and turned around.

"Duck!" said Jack.

The two of them hunched down.

After a long moment, they raised their heads. They peeked out again.

Dinosaurs
Before
Dark

"Coast clear," said Jack.

"Yay," whispered Annie.

"We have to get out of here," said Jack.

"You made a wish before," said Annie.

"I wish we could go back to Frog Creek," said Jack.

Nothing happened.

"I wish—"

"Wait. You were looking at a picture in the dinosaur book. Remember?"

The dinosaur book.

Jack groaned. "Oh, no. I left the book and my pack on the hill. I have to go back."

"Oh, forget it," said Annie.

"I can't," said Jack. "The book doesn't belong to us. Plus my notebook's in my pack. With all my notes."

"Hurry!" said Annie.

神奇树屋

MAGIC TREE HOUSE

Jack hurried down the rope ladder.

He leaped to the ground.

He raced past the Pteranodon, through the ferns, through the tall grass, and up the hill.

He looked down.

There was his pack, lying on the ground. On top of it was the dinosaur book.

But now the valley below was filled with Anatosauruses. All standing guard around the nests.

Where had they been? Did fear of the Tyrannosaurus send them home?

Jack took a deep breath.

Ready! Set! Go!

He charged down the hill. He leaped to his backpack. He scooped it up. He grabbed the dinosaur book.

A terrible tuba sound! Another! Another! All the Anat-

osauruses were bellowing at him.

Jack took off.

He raced up to the hilltop.

He started down the hill.

He stopped.

The Tyrannosaurus rex was back! And he was standing between Jack and the tree house!

A Giant Shadow

恐龙谷历险记
Dinosaurs
Before
Dark

Jack jumped behind the magnolia tree.

His heart was beating so fast he could hardly think.

He peeked out at the giant monster. The horrible-looking creature was opening and closing his huge jaws. His teeth were as big as steak knives.

Don't panic. Think.

Jack peered down at the valley.

Good. The duck-billed dinosaurs were sticking close to their nests.

Jack looked back at the Tyrannosaurus.

Good. The monster still didn't seem to know he was there.

Don't panic. Think. *Think.* Maybe there's information in the book.

Jack opened the dinosaur book. He found Tyranno-saurus rex. He read:

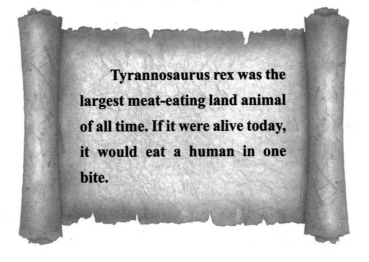

Tyrannosaurus rex was the largest meat-eating land animal of all time. If it were alive today, it would eat a human in one bite.

Great. The book was no help at all.

Okay. He couldn't hide on the other side of the hill. The Anatosauruses might stampede.

Okay. He couldn't run to the tree house. The Tyrannosaurus might run faster.

Okay. Maybe he should just wait. Wait for the monster to leave.

Jack peeked around the tree.

The Tyrannosaurus had wandered *closer* to the hill.

Something caught Jack's eye. Annie was coming down the rope ladder!

Was she nuts! What was she doing?

Jack watched Annie hop off the ladder.

She went straight to the Pteranodon. She was talking to him. She was flapping her arms. She pointed at Jack, at the sky, at the tree house.

She *was* nuts!

"Go! Go back up the tree!" Jack whispered. "Go!"

Suddenly Jack heard a roar.

The Tyrannosaurus rex was looking in his direction.

Jack hit the ground.

The Tyrannosaurus rex was coming toward the hill.

Jack felt the ground shaking.

神奇树屋

MAGIC TREE HOUSE

Should he run? Crawl back into Dinosaur Valley? Climb the magnolia tree?

Just then a giant shadow covered Jack. He looked up.

The Pteranodon was gliding overhead. The giant creature sailed down toward the top of the hill.

He was coming straight for Jack.

• 138 •

The Amazing Ride

神奇树屋
MAGIC TREE HOUSE

The Pteranodon coasted down to the ground.

He stared at Jack with his bright, alert eyes.

What was Jack supposed to do? Climb on? "But I'm too heavy," thought Jack.

Don't think. Just do it.

Jack looked at the Tyrannosaurus.

He was starting up the hill. His giant teeth were flashing in the sunlight.

Okay. Don't think. Just do it!

Jack put his book in his pack. Then he eased down onto the Pteranodon's back.

He held on tightly.

The creature moved forward. He spread out his wings—and lifted off the ground!

They teetered this way. Then that.

Jack nearly fell off.

The Pteranodon steadied himself, then rose into the sky.

Jack looked down. The Tyrannosaurus was chomping the air and staring up at him.

The Pteranodon glided away.

He sailed over the hilltop.

He circled over the valley. Over all the nests filled with babies. Over all the giant duck-billed dinosaurs.

Then the Pteranodon soared out over the plain— over the Triceratops who was grazing in the high grass.

It was amazing! It was a miracle!

Jack felt like a bird. As light as a feather.

The wind was rushing through his hair. The air smelled sweet and fresh.

He whooped. He laughed.

Jack couldn't believe it. He was riding on the back of an ancient flying reptile!

神奇 树 屋
MAGIC TREE HOUSE

The Pteranodon sailed over the stream, over the ferns and bushes.

Then he carried Jack down to the base of the oak tree.

When they came to a stop, Jack slid off the creature's back. And landed on the ground.

Then the Pteranodon took off again and glided into the sky.

"Bye, Henry," whispered Jack.

"Are you okay?" Annie shouted from the tree house.

Jack pushed his glasses into place. He kept staring up at the Pteranodon.

"Jack, are you okay?" Annie called.

Jack looked up at Annie. He smiled.

"Thanks for saving my life," he said. "That was really fun."

"Climb up!" said Annie.

恐龙谷历险记

Dinosaurs
Before
Dark

Jack tried to stand. His legs were wobbly.

He felt a bit dizzy.

"Hurry!" shouted Annie. "He's coming!"

Jack looked around. The Tyrannosaurus was heading straight toward him!

Jack bolted to the ladder. He grabbed the sides and started up.

"Hurry! Hurry!" screamed Annie.

Jack scrambled into the tree house.

"He's coming toward the tree!" Annie cried.

Suddenly something slammed against the oak tree. The tree house shook like a leaf.

Jack and Annie tumbled into the books.

"Make a wish!" cried Annie.

"We need the book! The one with the picture of Frog Creek!" said Jack. "Where is it?"

He pushed some books aside. He had to find that book about Pennsylvania.

There it was!

He grabbed it and tore through it, looking for the photograph of the Frog Creek woods.

He found it! Jack pointed to the picture.

"I wish we could go home!" he shouted.

The wind began to moan. Softly at first.

"Hurry!" Jack yelled.

The wind picked up. It was whistling now.

The tree house started to spin.

It spun faster and faster.

Jack closed his eyes. He held on tightly to Annie.

Then everything was still.

Absolutely still.

Home Before Dark

A bird began to sing.

Jack opened his eyes. He was still pointing at the picture of the Frog Creek woods.

He peeked out the tree house window. Outside he saw the exact same view.

"We're home," whispered Annie.

The woods were lit with a golden late-afternoon light. The sun was about to set.

No time had passed since they'd left.

"Ja-ack! An-nie!" a voice called from the distance.

"That's Mom," said Annie, Pointing.

Jack saw their mother far away. She was standing in front of their house. She looked very tiny.

"An-nie! Ja-ack!" she called.

Annie stuck her head out the window and shouted, "Come-ing!"

Jack still felt dazed. He just stared at Annie.

"What happened to us?" he said.

"We took a trip in a magic tree house," said Annie simply.

"But it's the same time as when we left," said Jack.

Annie shrugged.

"And how did it take us so far away?" said Jack. "And so long ago?"

"You just looked at a book and said you wished we could go there," said Annie. "And the magic tree house took us there."

"But *how?*" said Jack. "And who built this magic tree house? Who put all these books here?"

"A magic person, I guess," said Annie.

A magic person?

"Oh, look," said Jack. "I almost forgot about this." He

reached into his pocket and pulled out the gold medallion. "Someone lost this back there... in dinosaur land. Look, there's a letter M on it."

Annie's eyes got round. "You think *M* stands for *magic person?" she said.*

"I don't know," said Jack. "I just know someone went to that place before us."

"Ja-ack! An-nie!" came the distant cry again.

Annie poked her head out the window. "Come-ing!" she shouted.

Jack put the gold medallion back in his pocket.

He pulled the dinosaur book out of his pack. And put it back with all the

恐龙谷历险记
Dinosaurs
Before
Dark

other books.

Then he and Annie took one last look around the tree
house.

"Good-bye, house," whispered Annie.

Jack slung his backpack over his shoulder. He pointed
at the ladder.

Annie started down. Jack followed.

Seconds later they hopped onto the ground and started
walking out of the woods.

"No one's going to believe our story," said Jack.

"So let's not tell anyone," said Annie.

"Dad won't believe it," said Jack.

"He'll say it was a dream," said Annie.

"Mom won't believe it," said Jack.

"She'll say it was pretend,"

"My teacher won't believe it," said Jack.

"She'll say you're nuts," said Annie.

"We better not tell anyone," said Jack.

"I already said that," said Annie.

Jack sighed. "I think I'm starting to not believe it myself," he said.

They left the woods and started up the road toward their house.

As they walked past all the houses on their street, the trip to dinosaur time *did* seem more and more like a dream.

Only *this* world and *this* time seemed real.

Jack reached into his pocket. He clasped the gold medallion.

He felt the engraving of the letter M. It made Jack's fingers tingle.

Jack laughed. Suddenly he felt very happy.

He couldn't explain what had happened today. But he

knew for sure that their trip in the magic tree house had
been real.

Absolutely real.

"Tomorrow," Jack asid softly, "we'll go back to the
woods."

"Of coures," said Annie.

"And we'll climb up to the tree house," said Jack.

"Of course," said Annie.

"And we'll see what happens next," said Jack.

"Of coures," said Annie. "Race you! "

And they took off together, running for home.

图书在版编目（ＣＩＰ）数据

恐龙谷历险记:英、汉/(美)奥斯本著；蓝葆春,蓝纯译. —武汉:湖北少年儿童出版社,2010.3

（神奇树屋:典藏版）

书名原文:Dinosaurs Before Dark

ISBN 978－7－5353－4945－3

Ⅰ.恐… Ⅱ.①奥…②蓝…③蓝… Ⅲ.儿童文学—短篇小说—美国—现代—英、汉 Ⅳ.Ⅰ712.84

中国版本图书馆 CIP 数据核字(2010)第 047442 号

This translation published by arrangement with Random House Children's Books, a division of Random House, Inc.

Book #1-**Dinosaurs Before Dark** Text copyright ⓒ 1992 by Mary Pope Osborne

Magic Tree House™ is a trademark of Mary Pope Osborne, used under license.

著作权合同登记号:图字:17-2006-050

神奇树屋典藏版 1——恐龙谷历险记

原　　著:[美]玛丽·波·奥斯本
责任编辑:叶　珺
整体设计:一壹图文

出 品 人:李 兵
出版发行:湖北少年儿童出版社
经　销:新华书店湖北发行所
印　刷:孝感市三环印务有限责任公司

规　格:880×1230 1/32 5印张
印　次:2010年4月第1版 2012年5月第4次印刷
书　号:ISBN 978－7－5353－4945－3
定　价:14.00元

业务电话:(027)87679179 87679199
http://www.hbcp.com.cn